WHOOPS-THERE GOES JOE!

Miles Gibson

Illustrated by Neal Layton

MACMILLAN CHILDREN'S BOOKS

First published 2006 by Macmillan Children's Books
a division of Macmillan Publishers Limited
20 New Wharf Road, London N1 9RR
Basingstoke and Oxford
www.panmacmillan.com

Associated companies throughout the world

ISBN-13 978-1405-05516-1
ISBN-10 1-405-05516-2

Text copyright © Miles Gibson 2006
Illustrations copyright © Neal Layton 2006

The right of Miles Gibson and Neal Layton to be identified as the
author and illustrator of this work has been asserted by them in accordance
with the Copyright, Designs and Patents Act 1988.

1 3 5 7 9 8 6 4 2

A CIP catalogue record for this book is available from
the British Library.

Typeset by David Butler
Printed and bound in Great Britain by Mackays of Chatham plc, Kent

For Susan
M.G.

For Tommy Griffin
N.L.

Chapter 1

Archie Bodkin lived with his mother and
father in a small house in the big city.
He had a goldfish and a baby brother. He
called the goldfish Bodger. The name of
his baby brother was Joe.

Archie led a regular life.
He had regular baths and
regularly combed his hair,
owned a regulation lunch
box and regularly went to school.
"You have to stay regular," said his
mother and father, who made a habit of
giving people good advice.

Archie was as regular as clockwork.
Every evening, after homework, he liked
to sit down to watch TV. He watched

Captain Marvellous in Space and programmes containing animals. They were his regular favourites.

Joe – who was only two years old – watched anything he could find by flicking through the channels with the remote control. He liked all the cartoons, picture puzzles, adventures and comedies.

But magic shows starring Cyril the Clown were his particular favourites. Almost everyone agreed that Baby Joe watched too much TV.

The trouble began one day when Uncle Bernie paid a visit. Uncle Bernie lived in a house called the Jackdaw's Nest. He had a nose like a raspberry and whiskers sprouting from his ears. He lived with a telescope, a parrot and many gadgets

of his own invention. He'd invented a
talking toaster that shouted at you when
the toast was done, a rocket-propelled
skateboard and a pair of luminous
slippers that were easier to find if you
had to get out of bed in the dark.

Archie loved Uncle Bernie. But his mother and father disapproved of him.

"He's a bad influence on the boy," they used to tell each other sadly. "His inventions are extremely odd and he doesn't keep regular hours."

Chapter 2

The day the trouble began, Uncle Bernie
arrived at the house with a special
surprise for the family.

"What is it?" asked Archie as they
watched Uncle Bernie struggling through

the front door. He was pulling an enormous
parcel made from cardboard and held
together with tape and string.
"It's a television," said Uncle
Bernie proudly as he
unwrapped a strange
contraption with lots
of dials and buttons
and a screen the size
of a wardrobe door.
The Bodkins looked puzzled.

"We already have a television," explained Mr Bodkin.

Uncle Bernie laughed. "Yes, but this is one of my own invention. It has extra grommets and gizmos and plenty of whatsits and thingamajigs. It has an egg timer and a radio, a thermometer and an alarm clock. It has everything."

"It's certainly big," said Archie.

"Yes," said Uncle Bernie. "And it has two hundred channels. It's very educational."

Archie's mother and father looked doubtful. But they couldn't refuse a gift that was very educational.

"I'll show you how it works," Uncle Bernie told Archie. "Look. I've made a special remote control." He pulled a black plastic box from his pocket. The box was studded with lots of buttons. "You press the top buttons – red, blue and orange – to change the channels. And the middle buttons – purple, green and yellow – to

select the language. And the bottom
buttons – russet, rose and lavender – to
control the colour, contrast and volume."

He pressed several buttons
and the television crackled
and popped and glowed with a
brilliant light. They saw a lady explaining
in Swedish how to make a sponge cake.

Uncle Bernie changed the channel with
his special gadget. The sponge-
cake lady disappeared and
they saw a man in a
yellow bow tie, talking
about the ruins of Rome.

"That's very educational," agreed Mr and Mrs Bodkin.

"Yes," said Uncle Bernie. "I hope it gives you hours of pleasure." And he laughed as he hurried away, back to the Jackdaw's Nest in time to feed the parrot.

For the first few days they watched everything they could find on their new television. They watched classical dancing in Darjeeling and juggling in Japan. They

watched traffic news from Trinidad, the
weather forecast for Florida and a history
of Halifax, Nova Scotia. And then they
grew tired of the novelty and went back
to watching their regular programmes.

By the end of the week
they had all stopped
spending so much time
sitting in front of Uncle
Bernie's contraption . . .
except for Baby Joe.

14

Baby Joe just couldn't stop. Whenever Archie came home from school he'd find Baby Joe sitting on the floor watching the TV with his nose pressed against the enormous screen and his fingers playing with the buttons on the remote control.

Chapter 3

"Come and play with me," Archie said to Joe one Saturday afternoon. "There are caterpillars in the garden." He was searching for his magnifying glass in the cupboard.

Baby Joe looked at Archie and grinned. He liked caterpillars. But he shook his head. He was watching television.

Archie went into the garden when their mother came into the room. She looked at Baby Joe and said, "Come into the kitchen. I'll make you some strawberry milk."

Joe looked up at his mother and grinned. He liked strawberry milk. But he shook his head. He was watching television.

Mrs Bodkin went back to the kitchen, where Mr Bodkin was eating a sandwich. "I'm worried about our baby," she said. "He watches too much TV."

"Everyone likes TV," said Mr Bodkin, brushing crumbs from his cardigan. He still liked to watch the football on

Wednesday nights and he knew his wife enjoyed watching people gardening on a Sunday afternoon. There was nothing wrong with that. He couldn't see the harm in it.

"But Joe is just a baby. When he grows up he'll have square eyes. It can't be healthy. I think you should talk to him."

Mr Bodkin sighed, wiped the butter from his moustache and walked into the living room.

Joe was still sitting on the floor watching TV with his nose pressed against the screen.

"Hello," said Mr Bodkin. "Would you like me to read you a story?"

Joe looked up at his father and grinned. He liked his father reading stories. But he shook his head. He was watching television.

Mr Bodkin frowned.

"If you sit too close to the screen, one day the TV will swallow you up," he warned. And he scooped Joe from the floor and put him beneath his arm.

"We'll sit together," said Mr Bodkin as he found a book and settled down in his favourite armchair. He placed Joe beside him in the cushions and began to read him a story.

But it was a warm afternoon and Mr Bodkin – who had eaten several sandwiches – yawned and fell asleep. He began to snore, and the storybook fell from his hand.

Baby Joe was soon feeling bored and uncomfortable. He wriggled and squirmed. He climbed down from the chair and crawled back to the big TV set. He clapped his hands in delight at the grommets and gizmos; blew bubbles at the whatsits and thingamajigs.

He looked at the screen, where a walrus was dancing with a polar bear. The bear wore a pair of spectacles. The walrus was waving a bowler hat.

Joe sat on the carpet and stared. "Woo-woo!" he said to the walrus. "Woo-woo!"

He pressed his hands against the screen and laughed. "Boo-boo!" he said to the bear. "Boo-boo!"

Then he picked up Uncle Bernie's special remote control and started to play with the buttons. There was a crackle and a flash and a loud whoosh – and then nothing at all but the sound of Mr Bodkin snoring . . .

Chapter 4

"Where's Joe?" said Archie when he came back from the garden after looking at caterpillars through his magnifying glass. He stared around the room, but Baby Joe was nowhere to be seen.

Mr Bodkin woke up with a snort and Mrs Bodkin gave a shriek and came running from the kitchen. "What have you done with our baby?" she demanded, frowning at her husband.

"He was sitting here a minute ago," complained Mr Bodkin. He stood up and glared at the chair, as if he thought it might be playing stupid tricks on him and hiding the baby behind its cushions.

"I can't leave you alone for five minutes," said Mrs Bodkin.

"Look!" said Archie.

"What?" cried Mrs Bodkin.

"There!" said Archie.

"Where?" shouted Mr Bodkin.

"He's inside the TV set!"

At first they didn't believe it. They gathered very close around the enormous screen and stared.

"My baby!" shrieked Mrs Bodkin.

Now they could see Baby Joe, sprawled on his back, looking rather confused and covered in snow while a walrus and a polar bear danced around him.

No wonder Joe looked confused. One
moment he'd been playing with the
buttons on the special TV remote, then –
whoops – before he'd had time to shout,
he'd dropped the control and been sucked
through the TV screen as if the glass was
as soft as a rainbow. One moment

he had been sitting on
the warm carpet, looking
at a winter wonderland
on TV – and the next

he was stranded on a block of ice, with snowflakes falling around him. The sky was black and the stars were shining.

Joe shivered, sat up and rubbed his head.

The walrus and the polar bear stopped dancing when they saw the little visitor. They bent down and peered at him.

"Hello, what's this?" said the walrus.

"It looks like a baby," said the polar bear, wiping the snow from his spectacles.

The walrus scratched his whiskers.

"That's strange. He shouldn't be out
alone in the cold. What are we going to
do with him?"

"I don't know," said the polar bear.

"Can you see his mother anywhere?" asked the walrus.

"No." The polar bear shook his head. "I can't see anything in these glasses."

They were quiet for a moment.

"Let's pretend it's not happening," suggested the walrus.

"Good idea!" said the polar bear.

And they walked away, arm in arm, for a mug of hot tea and a fried-egg sandwich.

Joe continued to sit on the ice with the snow gently drifting over his head. He wasn't dressed for the cold. His fingers were turning blue. His breath hung like steam in the frosty air.

"They've left him alone in the snow!" said Archie indignantly.

"What are you going to do to save him?" shouted Mrs Bodkin, glaring at

her husband. She blamed Mr Bodkin
for the accident.

"Switch off the TV!" shouted Mr
Bodkin. "Pull out the plug! We'll soon
stop this nonsense!" He was going to
find his screwdriver set and take
the television apart.

"No," cried Archie.
"If we switch it off
we might lose
Baby Joe forever."

35

"That's right," said Mrs Bodkin. "How can you be so heartless?"

"Well, we can't stand here like lemons," grumbled Mr Bodkin.

"I think we should call Uncle Bernie," said Archie. And he hurried away to phone the Jackdaw's Nest.

Chapter 5

Uncle Bernie wasted no time in rushing back to the house. He stared at Baby Joe still trapped inside the TV set and then stared at the remote control left behind on the carpet. He frowned and scratched his head. "I think he pressed 'Enter' by mistake," he said at last.

"Enter?" said Archie.

"Yes," said Uncle Bernie.

"Why would that make him enter the TV set?" asked Mr Bodkin. "It sounds very irregular to me."

"I don't know," said Uncle Bernie. "It's a mystery of science." He shook the remote control and heard a nasty rattle. "There must be something wrong with one of the connections."

"Well, what are you going to do to get our baby home again?" said Mrs Bodkin.

Uncle Bernie looked worried. He pressed a few buttons, hoping the problem would solve itself. Baby Joe grew large and then small and then went back to his normal size; he turned red and then green and then went back to his usual colour, but he was still on the wrong side of the television screen.

"I think we should try to move him into a different sort of programme," suggested Archie.

"What sort of programme?" asked Uncle Bernie.

"One without snow," said Archie.

"And how would that help?" demanded Mr Bodkin.

"At least he'd be warm and dry while we think about how to rescue him," explained Archie. He was eight years old and full of bright ideas.

"Quite right!" said Uncle Bernie. "We shouldn't leave him out in the cold."

"But how do we do it?" Mrs Bodkin wanted to know.

"We'll try the remote control again," said Archie. "Perhaps we can move Joe into a different programme when we press the buttons to change the channels."

"It might work!" said Uncle Bernie.

So Archie took the gadget and pressed the buttons. He was looking for his favourite show.

"There!" said Archie, as the television crackled and changed channels. "It's *Captain Marvellous in Space*. You can always trust Captain Marvellous in an emergency."

They watched the screen. Captain Marvellous had been on a mission to the moon in six exciting episodes. Now he

was getting ready to blast off to the stars
in his Marvellous Galaxy Cruiser.

"Whoops – there goes Joe!" cried Mrs
Bodkin as they saw their baby appear
at the top of the screen and then
drop, with a thump,
between the
Captain's shiny
space boots.

Joe sat up and
blinked. He was

still covered in snow. But when he saw Captain Marvellous, he smiled.

"Woo-woo!" he said to Captain Marvellous.

Marvellous hadn't seen the visitor – he was busy getting ready for another of his famous adventures.

"He'll be safe with the Captain while we try to come up with a rescue plan," said Archie confidently.

But moments before the Captain fired

the rocket engines, he glanced down and
saw the baby.

"Hello," he said. "How did you get
here? We can't have babies blasting
off into space. I'll leave you out for
your mother."

He opened the hatch
and placed Joe on
the ground like an
empty milk bottle
on a doorstep.

Joe was so surprised that he didn't have time to complain. When the rocket engines were fired he was blown into the air and found himself tumbling head over heels towards a deep and dusty crater.

"Stop!" shouted Mr Bodkin as Captain Marvellous shot off towards the stars. "You're leaving our baby boy on the moon."

He lost his temper and banged the TV with his fist.

"Getting angry won't save our baby from disappearing into a crater," Mrs Bodkin reminded him.

"Quick!" said Archie. "There's still time. I think we can save him by changing the programme."

He pressed another button on the remote control. The television crackled and changed channels.

"Don't put him with any wild animals," Mrs Bodkin warned her son as he started flicking through the programmes again. "Be sure to choose something suitable. You never know what you'll find on TV."

"Who's that idiot?" said Uncle Bernie suddenly.

"That's Cyril the Magic Clown," said

Archie as they stared at a man wearing red pantaloons and a pair of long rubber shoes.

Every afternoon, Cyril the Magic Clown performed hilarious conjuring tricks with the help of his lovely assistant, Janet. Sometimes he juggled with custard pies and sometimes he balanced a chair on his nose. Today he was planning to shoot strings of coloured handkerchiefs from the barrel of his magic cannon.

"Whoops – there goes Joe!" said Mrs Bodkin as they saw their baby appear at the top of the screen.

"He'll be safe with Cyril while we try to come up with a rescue plan," said Archie confidently. "He's Baby Joe's favourite character."

But Cyril hadn't seen Baby Joe. And when Baby Joe dropped into the show, he dropped straight down the barrel of the magic cannon.

"Boo-hoo," he said
in the dark. But his voice
was muffled and no one
heard him.

"Stop!" shouted Mr
Bodkin at the TV set.
"You can't shoot our
baby from your magic
cannon." He was
still very angry and
red in the face.

51

Cyril the Magic Clown struck a match and lit the fuse to fire the cannon while his lovely assistant played the trumpet and turned circles on silver roller skates.

"We'll never get him back again," sobbed Mrs Bodkin, wiping her eyes on her kitchen apron.

Archie looked at his father shouting and his mother sobbing and the fuse burning down in the cannon and he knew that he had to do something fast and he knew

that he had to do something drastic.

"I have another idea," he said. "If I can follow Baby Joe into the TV set, I might be able to keep him safe and out of mischief."

"And how are you going to get home again?" grumbled his father.

"I don't know," said Archie. "But Joe's too small to help himself and if we don't do something very soon that cannon will fire him through the ceiling."

"How are you going to get into the TV set?" asked his mother.

"Well, if I hold the remote control very tight and press 'Enter' . . ." said Archie hopefully.

"I don't recommend it," said Uncle Bernie.

"We don't know what will happen," said his mother.

"It might go wrong," said his father.

But it was too late. Before anyone could

stop him, Archie had pointed the gadget
at the TV and pressed the forbidden
button.

Chapter 6

There was a crackle and a flash as Archie felt himself stretched and squeezed and lifted clean from the carpet. He was dragged forward in a loud whoosh and sucked through the TV screen. It didn't hurt.

It happened too quickly.

When he opened his eyes, Archie found himself standing on the stage behind Cyril's lovely assistant. The remote control was still clutched in his hand.

The lovely assistant looked surprised but, thinking Archie must be part of the act, she blew on her trumpet and skated around him in circles.

At that very moment there was a loud bang, a plume of fluttering handkerchiefs and Baby Joe shot from the cannon.

Archie closed his eyes and threw out
his hands. Baby Joe flew through the
air . . . and dropped into Archie's arms.
Archie was so surprised he'd caught him
that he fell in a heap on the floor.

"Boo-boo," laughed Joe, and he blew a bubble. He was very pleased to see his big brother.

"Hello," said Archie when he'd recovered.

But Cyril the Clown looked angry. He blamed Archie for spoiling his trick.

"Hold tight," said Archie as he put Joe down, grabbed his hand and pressed the buttons on the remote control.

"Stop!" shouted Cyril.

The television crackled and changed channels as Cyril stamped towards them in his long rubber shoes . . . and vanished.

Archie and his baby brother found themselves tumbling slowly, head over heels, towards a sunlit ocean until they landed on the deck of a sailing ship. They could hear the waves splashing beneath them and canvas creaking above their heads as the wind caught in the sails.

"Whoops," said Archie as he sat up and rubbed his head. "This doesn't look very suitable. I think it's a pirate ship."

He was staring at a fierce-looking character with a black eyepatch and

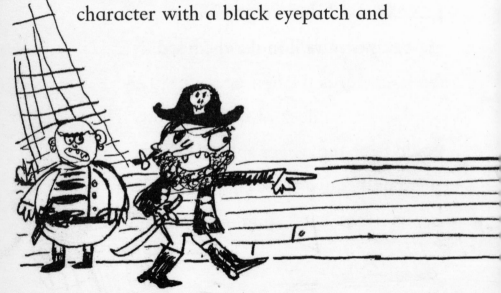

a ginger beard. He wore high boots
and carried a cutlass in his belt.

"Stowaways!" roared the pirate
captain when he saw Archie and Baby
Joe. "We can't have stowaways stealing
the biscuits – we'll make them walk
the plank!"

A fat pirate with silver earrings and gold teeth rushed forward and seized Archie and Joe by their collars. He bundled them to the end of the plank.

"Hold tight!" said Archie as he glanced down at the ocean beneath them. He squeezed Baby Joe's hand. "We're leaving. We have to find someone sensible who is going to take us home."

"Jump!" shouted the pirate captain. "You're going overboard."

Archie pressed the
buttons on the
remote control.

The television
crackled and changed
channels as the fat pirate lunged
forward to give Archie a nasty prod with
his cutlass . . . and vanished.

Archie and his baby brother went
tumbling head over heels until they
found themselves slowly sinking towards

dry land again. But
now it was dark and
the moon was shining.
They could smell wood smoke
and hear someone playing the harmonica.
"Whoops," said Archie as he sat up
and looked around. "This doesn't look
very helpful. I think we've landed in the
Wild West."
He was staring at a circle of cowboys
sitting around an open campfire. The

cowboys had leather waistcoats and big moustaches. They wore ten-gallon hats and carried six-shooters in their belts. They were busy cooking their supper when Archie and Joe dropped in on them.

"Rustlers!" growled one of the cowboys when he saw Archie and Baby Joe. He waved his fork in a threatening manner.

67

"Catch them quick – they'll be trying to rustle our pork and beans."

The cowboys looked angry – they were obviously hungry. One of them jumped up and pulled a lasso from his saddlebag. He glared at Archie and Joe as he started to spin the rope, faster and faster, over his head.

"Hold tight!" said Archie as he saw the lasso flying towards them. He squeezed Baby Joe's hand. "We're leaving again."

"Gotcha!" shouted the cowboy as the
lasso caught Archie and Joe in its noose.

Archie pressed the buttons on
the remote control.

The cowboy pulled
hard on the rope,
dragging Archie and
Joe towards him. The
television crackled and changed
channels as the cowboy made a grab
for his captives . . . and vanished.

Archie and his baby brother went tumbling head over heels until they found themselves at last sinking through a studio ceiling.

"This looks more promising," said Archie. There were lights and cameras and far below he could see a woman with big hair, who was reading the six o'clock TV news. She looked very sensible. She wore a blue jacket and dangly earrings.

She spoke about a politician who was

worried about the price of carrots, a film
star who had written a book and a poodle
winning first prize at a famous dog show.

"And that's the end of the news," she said.

She was just getting ready to read the
weather report when Archie and Joe
landed with a tremendous thump on her desk.

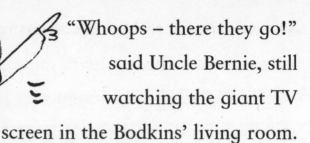

"Whoops – there they go!"
said Uncle Bernie, still
watching the giant TV
screen in the Bodkins' living room.

Baby Joe sat up and sneezed. He looked
dirty and lost and rather frightened.
When he saw the woman with big
hair he burst into tears.

"Boo-hoo!" he said
to the woman.

The woman said nothing.

72

She was meant to be forecasting rain, but when she saw the intruders she was so surprised that she clutched her throat as if she'd swallowed a tennis ball. Her dangly earrings started to tremble.

"I'm sorry," said Archie politely. "We didn't mean to frighten you."

"I've had enough of this nonsense!" Mr Bodkin shouted at the TV set.

"Someone save my baby!" pleaded Mrs Bodkin.

And then, as they watched, a man with headphones dashed forward, grabbed Archie and Joe from the newsdesk and hurried them from the picture.

"They've vanished," gasped Mr Bodkin.

"Where have they gone?" cried Mrs Bodkin.

"Don't ask me," said Uncle Bernie impatiently. "I don't know everything."

Chapter 7

The man with headphones had taken Archie and Joe to the office of an important executive.

The important executive wanted to know what had happened to upset the six o'clock news. It was a serious state of affairs.

Archie tried to explain how Baby Joe had got lost inside the TV set.

"That was very careless," said the important man.

"Yes," agreed Archie. "We'll be more careful in future. Now, I wonder if you could kindly put us in a taxi and send us home to 12 Hazelnut Avenue."

At seven o'clock that evening, a taxi

stopped at 12 Hazelnut Avenue and the
important man from the television studio
rang the doorbell and gave Archie and Joe
back to their parents.

"Here is your baby," he said.

"Thank you," said Mrs Bodkin.

"And here's Archie," said
the important man,
"who deserves a
medal for helping
to save Baby Joe."

"We're very grateful. Thank you for bringing them home," said Mr Bodkin.

"Don't mention it," said the important man. "But please don't let it happen again. I'm very important. I have a large desk and several telephones. I don't have time to chase children."

"It won't happen again," promised Mrs Bodkin as she took Baby Joe away for a whoopsie, a wash and clean pyjamas.

"This is our fault," said Mr Bodkin when the important man from the TV studio had gone. "We have only ourselves to blame. In future we must pick our programmes carefully and watch television as a family."

"That's very sensible," said Mrs Bodkin.

"And I think we had better return to watching our old TV," Archie told Uncle Bernie sadly. "I don't think your new invention was properly invented."

"You're probably right," said Uncle Bernie. "Perhaps there were too many grommets and gizmos."

Everyone agreed with him.

So they helped Uncle Bernie unplug his big contraption and take it back to the Jackdaw's Nest.

That evening the Bodkins sat together to watch their old TV from a safe distance. They had hot chocolate and sultana biscuits. While they watched, Mrs Bodkin took up her knitting, Mr Bodkin picked up the paper and started doing a crossword puzzle, and Archie looked through the pictures in his favourite caterpillar book.

"We're watching TV as a family,"
Archie told his baby brother.

But Joe – who was tired from his
adventures – had already fallen asleep.

The End

The End

Another Little Archie adventure

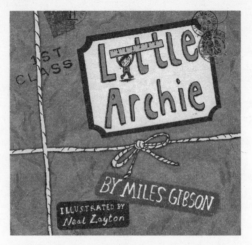

It all begins with barmy Uncle Bernie
and a birthday bottle of shrinking powder.
One taste and Archie becomes just three inches
tall – or should that be small? – and tiny enough
to be popped in the post . . .

A perfectly parcelled adventure –
a gift for readers big and small!